THE EIGHT

CONNOR WHITELEY

No part of this book may be reproduced in any form or by any electronic or mechanical means. Including information storage, and retrieval systems, without written permission from the author except for the use of brief quotations in a book review.

This book is NOT legal, professional, medical, financial or any type of official advice.

Any questions about the book, rights licensing, or to contact the author, please email connorwhiteley@connorwhiteley.net

Copyright © 2023 CONNOR WHITELEY

All rights reserved.

DEDICATION
Thank you to all my readers without you I couldn't do what I love.

CHAPTER 1

Assassin Sophia Russel had always hated Mars with a passion. As far as she was concerned it was nothing more than a massive chunk of red rock filled with dust, dust and more dust. Well that wasn't exactly true because they were plenty of idiots there.

Sophia pressed her rubber-suited back against the biting cold metal of a nearby habitat-block that rose up high into the orange sky like it would give its inhabitants plenty of room to live, make love and enjoy life.

But that was far from how Mars worked for normal people, Sophia was more than glad she didn't have to live here. She only had to kill here. Sophia just hated how all those rooms in the block would be so small, damp and cramp. Yet that was the thing about Mars, no one lived here, only mindless drones worked here.

Sophia watched everyone else walk up and down the little metal street made of dirty grey metal as hard workers who looked like they were about to kilt over hurried back and forth to their habitat blocks for one reason or another.

Even the air was disgusting and Sophia just wanted to have her kill and be done with this damn planet. The air was filled with so-called delightful hints of oil, burnt rubber and other toxic fumes that Sophia seriously didn't want to think about. She was just glad her high-tech rubber assassin suit, that looked like normal clothing under her cloak, was managing to filter out most of the toxins. It was just a shame it wasn't all of them.

Sophia really wished she was still back on Earth, the amazing birthcraddle of humanity with the rest of her kill team preparing for a mission, but she was sadly here. Here on an idiotic world that she would happily burn to the ground if she was ordered to.

It wasn't so much that Sophia hated the planet, it was more the leaders and the purpose of Mars. Mars was thankfully one of the best forge worlds in the entire Great Human Empire and Sophia respected it for that. She had been to plenty of these amazing worlds that were dedicated solely to the production of weapons, armour and vehicles for the war machine known as the Great Human Empire.

Sophia had no problem with that purpose of Mars.

The real problem was the leaders of Mars were nobs. Plain and simple. Dickheads might have been a better way to put it but Sophia still hated the punch in the face she had gotten from her hard-ass superior for making such a so-called silly comment. But those leaders really were.

The eight people in charge of Mars were some of the most powerful people in the entire Empire, and those eight idiots knew it. They knew if they desired something they could summon Earth and they would have to be given it in fear of Mars ordering all the hundreds of thousands of Forge worlds across the entire Empire to stop production.

Sure it would take weeks to get the message to every Forge world and then maybe another week for the worlds to shut down (you cannot simply turn off an entire planet), but Sophia had always been interested if anyone had the balls to actually do it.

The Emperor had no interest in appeasing Mars so the Eight had never tested their luck, but everyone knew it was only a matter of time. Sophia guessed it would happen in the next few weeks so... things needed to change and she was happy to change them.

One of the Eight needed to die.

The sound of the vast factories in the distance hammering, popping and roaring echoed around the entire planet and Sophia was glad soon this planet would be a little safer and a little more loyal to the Emperor. Especially with an Anti-Empire member of the Eight about to die, and if everything went according to, which when Sophia did it her plans normally did, he should be replaced with a more Pro-Empire member.

In all honesty Sophia didn't particularly care too much but as long as herself, her kill team and her Emperor were safe, she would keep doing what she was told. And she could hardly deny her so-called work (more like play) wasn't great fun and pleasurable at times.

The sound of a metal leg hitting the metal ground very hard made Sophia simply smile and get really excited. She was far too highly trained for her heart to race, her breathing to increase or even sweat. She was just excited about the kill.

Sophia slowly looked up as she saw her target. Forge Captain General O'Neil was definitely not a humanoid anymore with his eight metal spider legs that looked like they had naturally grown out of his metal waist. Each leg had an extremely sharp and deadly point to them.

Sophia was looking forward to this show.

O'Neil even moved like a stupid spider as his bulky legs tried to move down the little street where Sophia was standing.

But what really interested Sophia was the bright red cloak covering the Forge Captain General's metallic body and his cold metal face. For O'Neil no longer had any human eyes or flesh for they had all been replaced with awful machines and cybernetics, burning away all of his humanity in the process.

Sophia hated the disgusting look of him and she seriously wanted him dead as he carefully eased his way past her. He didn't even look at her and considering it was Machine Day, the weird-ass equivalent to a Martian Holy Day where they were meant to pay respect to those of flesh and blood who were apparently less fortunate, Sophia was hardly impressed.

"Have you come to kill me then?" O'Neil said, his voice harsh, computerised and lacking any hint of humanity.

Sophia didn't react.

"I wondered when the Empire would seek to eliminate me," he said. "I must admit assassin. My calculations were wrong for a change. I did not calculate you would dare kill me a Martian on Machine Day,"

Sophia pretended not to hear him, but she

loosened her wrists for when she needed to attack, when she needed to activate her holographic swords and kill him.

"This is why Mars should be ruling the Empire and not the Weaklings of Flesh. It is your kind that was damning the species. That is the real point of Machine Day to remind us superior being how weak, pathetic and worthless you Fleshings are,"

He swung his legs at Sophia.

Sophia flicked her wrists. Two blue swords appeared in her hands.

Sophia swung her swords.

Slicing through two of his legs.

He hissed. He groaned. He shrieked.

Six metal legs swung at her.

Throwing her against the wall.

Slashing her chest.

Sophia swung her sword.

Slicing into another leg.

O'Neil hissed.

Sophia charged.

Jumping into the air.

O'Neil was quick. Five lashing legs swung at Sophia.

She dropped. Dodging most of them.

She rolled forward.

One leg smashed down on her. Trapping one of her legs.

Sophia was pinned. She couldn't move. She couldn't escape.

O'Neil whacked Sophia closer to him.

Sophia just smiled as O'Neil towered over her and was so sure she was going to die. Sophia noticed he was only standing on three legs, the surviving four and a half were all aimed at her. Yet O'Neil was too calculating, too precise, too clever (apparently) to leave anything to chance and he had already calculated her options for escape most probably.

Normally Sophia would charge right at him and use her assassin speed to kill him before his legs even got close to touching her.

But he would have guessed that.

Sophia supposed her next option would be to run to one of the legs he was standing on and slice it. Making him unstable and collapse. Catch him off guard so to speak.

He would have guessed that too.

Sophia seriously wasn't even going to consider the stupidity of attacking the three legs aimed at her. That was suicide plain and simple.

She was out of options.

So there was always only going to be one option left that Sophia absolutely hated, but she would hate dying a lot more. She would hate not being able to serve her Emperor a few more times and she would seriously hate not being able to see her Kill Team one final time.

Sophia had to run away.

She rolled backwards.

The metal legs shot forward.

They thought she had gone forward.

O'Neil was stupid.

The metal legs slammed into the floor.

Breaking it.

The legs tried to move.

They were stuck.

Sophia jumped up.

The metal legs were stuck. O'Neil looked unstable. He was about to fall over.

He was trying too hard to free his legs.

Sophia charged.

Jumping onto the trapped legs.

Jumping off them.

Raising her swords. Swinging them.

Slashing the metallic throat of O'Neil.

As black oily blood splashed against the biting cold walls of the habitat block, Sophia carefully landed on the ground and beheaded O'Neil. There was no chance she would ever risk him being alive.

That was not an option.

Then for good measure and because Sophia loved this part, she spilled his black oily cables that had replaced his stomach and guts long ago. There was absolutely no chance O'Neil was alive now.

He was as dead as his own humanity.

Sophia just smiled at herself and knew that she had done more than enough today for her Empire and finally a Pro-Empire member of Mars could be ever so carefully guided into the ranks of the Eight and Mars's loyalty to the Emperor could be reaffirmed.

As the sound of the vast factories in the distance hammering, popping and roaring became noticeable again, Sophia just frowned and she seriously hated Mars, and she was just glad she was never going to have to return to this Emperor-forsaken rock again.

CHAPTER 2

Assassin Novice Victor Istanbul had never really known why he had chosen to join the assassin temples, learn and train to become an Assassin. His entire family and friends back on his backwater planet that he called home had been shocked. They were outraged for the most part, but Victor just felt like it was his calling.

As he sat in the very bright, spacious apartment that was perfectly rectangular in shape, Victor just focused on the pleasurably warm feeling pulsing through his body as he sat on the specially designed stools around a large white kitchen table made of crystal.

If anyone had told him that was what assassins ate around in the morning he would have called them liars. Victor had always imagined assassins to lurk in deep dark caves and lairs where the heads and corpses and blood of their victims would be the decorate.

But he had clearly been flat out wrong as the

communal apartment he shared with the other two members of the kill team was large, very bright and there wasn't even a hint of death in the air.

In fact Victor had never smelt air so fresh, crisp and marvellous as the air in the apartment. Victor doubted the vast majority of people on Earth had access to the high-tech pumps and filters and that made the air so clean.

The lack of good quality air was one of the first things Victor had actually noticed about Earth when he first arrived wet with blood from his training on the assassin ships. The air of Earth was so polluted, thick with toxins and just awful that Victor was surprised people lived here as long as they did.

The sound of people muttering, talking and whispering behind Victor made him smile a little. He might have only been in the kill team for a month and a complete novice but he did love his friends.

And as much as the other two and that beautiful Sophia tried to give him the hard shoulder for being a newbie, he just knew they wanted the best for him.

Victor returned to the large blue bowl of porridge with spoonfuls of custard, extra vitamins and protein stirred in. Everything an assassin needed to kill the enemies of the Emperor.

Victor stuck another spoonful in his mouth and wow, this stuff from the replicator was just brilliant. Sure replicators, Argi-worlds and hydroponic farms were the only ways to get food in the Empire, but the replicators on Victor's homeworld were rubbish compared to this.

The amazing softness of the oats, creaminess of the milk and that sweet spicy bite of the cinnamon was just sheer perfection. Victor was so glad he could have as much of this as he desired.

"Morning Vic!" a woman shouted behind him.

Victor waved to Addison as she spoke into the air what she wanted (it was the same as Victor's breakfast) and it appeared just opposite Victor.

Addison pulled over a stool and Victor smiled at her. He had always loved her stunningly smooth face, long brown hair and killer eyes that he was fairly sure would kill him if he stared too long.

"Victor," a man said coldly as he got the same breakfast as the other two.

Victor nodded to Dexter in his long black trench coat, black boots and his bald head as he sat down at the table.

Dexter just sneered at Victor. Victor actually had no idea why Dexter didn't like him in the slightest, but he had clearly done something wrong to upset him. But then again that sexy Sophia had mentioned that Dexter was just cold and moody and awful most of the time.

Maybe he really shouldn't worry about it too much.

"Sophia's returning today, right?" Victor asked.

Addison looked like she was about to speak but Dexter waved her silent.

"That is no matter of yours. She is our leader and

she shouldn't have anything to do with you," he said.

Victor wanted to remind him he had been the sole survivor of his section of the assassin training on the ships. He had killed the twenty of other (considerably more) trained novices and he survived.

But that was the last thing he was going to do, the last thing he wanted Dexter to do was challenge him to a fight. Victor seriously didn't like his odds there.

"Yes," Addison said. "She'll be returning today to us. She left Mars two weeks ago but apparently she got sent off on two more missions. Turns out Mars has a lot of hatred towards the Emperor,"

Victor just couldn't believe why Mars would be like this, he had studied the history of the Empire (both the official and unofficial) at school and later at university. Mars was treated so well by the Emperor and the Council of Mars had always had the Emperor's respect and ear, so it just made absolutely no sense why they would hate the Empire.

"Kill them all is what I say," Dexter said eating his porridge.

"That's illegal," Victor said.

Dexter and Addison laughed.

"Empire Laws do not apply to us," Dexter said. "We are the lawless blade of the Empire. We can and shall kill whoever threatens the Empire,"

Victor wanted to argue. Sure that was the literal definition of how the assassins were meant to work, but it seemed so wrong.

Victor was just grateful the vast majority of the assassins had morality to guide them, but he wasn't so sure if Dexter was one of them.

"What are the chances of a full-scale rebellion from Mars?" Victor said, taking another amazing bite of his breakfast.

"You know," Addison said, "a lot more likely than you think. The council is officially designed to always have Pro-Empire members on it, but that hasn't happened for some time,"

"So now the pathetic Emperor's Council allow Mars to have a maximum of four Anti-Empire members as The Eight," Dexter said. "They should all die is what I think,"

Victor wasn't sure if the Emperor's Council that governed the entire Great Human Empire was pathetic, but it did seem like an error of judgement. Victor firmly believed that no one who despises the Empire should be allowed to have power, but clearly others didn't think so.

"But why kill them all?" Victor asked. "That makes no sense. If you kill them all and impose direct rule then that stretches the Empire's resources even more. Can we really afford that?"

Dexter whipped out a dagger, placing it on the table.

"We are assassins," he said. "I don't give two shits about the politics, resources or fuck knows what of the Empire. I just kill the enemy before they can kill us,"

Addison looked like something disturbed her then she pulled out a little dataslate and smiled.

"Sophia is coming back up now," she said.

Victor just beamed. This was going to be amazing, he really wanted to see that bright sexy woman again, who could and would almost kill him in a second.

"We will finish this conversation another time idiot," Dexter said. "And please don't say embarrassing stuff in front of Sophia. It only makes you seem even more pathetic than you already are,"

Victor was so determined to complete his training, training as hard as he could and become a better assassin than Dexter ever could. And that was far, far from a threat, it was a promise to himself and his Emperor.

The sound of the apartment door opening made Victor's stomach fill with little butterflies.

"How was Mars?" Addison asked.

Sophia walked straight to the table. "It was shit as always. And now they're rebelling against us,"

All three of them dropped their spoons. They weren't hungry now.

Victor didn't want to admit how much that terrified him.

CHAPTER 3

The wonderful, rich, thick smell of creamy custard-filled porridge filled Sophia's senses as she stood at the large kitchen table in the assassin apartment. It was so perfectly amazing to see her beloved kill team again, Sophia hadn't actually realised til now how much she had missed them.

But of course she was never going to tell them that, she didn't want them to think she was going soft on them.

Sophia could only subtly stare at Victor as he sat there on his stool wearing his skin-tight assassin suit, like her, filled with its wide range of little gadgets to help them out in the field.

Victor looked so beautiful and sexy in his suit. Thankfully it led so little to the imagination that Sophia was so tempted to spend the night with him and trace her long killer fingers all over his sexy rock hard abs.

Sophia had to focus. She couldn't think like this.

She had a kill team and mission to lead.

The clean, crisp, refreshing hints of the air was such a breath of fresh air considering Sophia had spent the past two weeks on Mars killing two more targets that had been considerably harder to track down, and what she gleamed from their deaths only worried her more than she ever wanted to admit.

It seemed that Mars was preparing to break away from the Empire. Not to such a foul extent that they were thinking of joining the traitors that wanted to burn down the Empire and replace the Emperor with its foul, evil tyrant of a leader.

But them separating from the Empire would cause so many delays getting ships, weapons and vehicles to battlefields and planets. That it would eventually grind the Empire to a halt, all whilst the enemies of the Empire kept on fighting.

This would spell the end of the Empire and the death of trillions, and Sophia was never going to allow that to happen.

What made it even worse was that Sophia hated the fact that it would inspire other worlds to do the same. Effectively cutting off important trading routes, recruitment grounds of the military and Agri-worlds that feed the Empire.

Sophia had to act and thankfully she knew her team was going to help her. She quickly explained to them the implications of it all.

"How did you find out about this plan?" Victor asked.

Dexter huffed. Sophia hated how he always dismissed everything Victor said or asked.

"My first target after killing O'Neil was a major Martian General who was amassing enough ships to launch an attack on Earth," Sophia said.

Everyone at the table looked concerned.

"It turned out the General was amassing them because he knew of the plot to separate from the Empire and was worried about the Empire sending forces to destroy Mars,"

"Like they bloody well should," Dexter said.

"Dexter-" Sophia said.

"No," he said. "We have had to deal with Mars and its arrogance for too long. It is about time we remind those idiots who is in charge around here,"

"That will only breed more hate and anger," Victor said coldly.

Dexter gestured to punch him. Addison just kept on eating her porridge.

"Enough Dexter," Sophia said coldly. "Then after that target was killed, I had to deal with the Martian governor,"

A very loud groan came from everyone at the table, and Sophia seriously couldn't blame them. She was still rather surprised to know the Governor was meant to make sure Mars and its forge worlds were complying with the law, Earth's directives and double checking that no traitors were infecting Mars. Sophia never would have guessed that considering it was the Governor who was lying to Earth, and personally funding the Anti-Empire operations.

"I snapped his neck in his office, but I found some blueprints of the main *Solar De Costa Space Port* on Mars. All the structural points on the blueprints were circled, so I believe he was planning a terror attack,"

Addison started scrapping her bowl like she was never going to eat again, and as much Sophia hated the noise as an assassin she might be right.

"What's the plan?" Dexter asked.

"We have been ordered to investigate the possible terror attack, assassinate its leader and most importantly stop Mars from separating,"

Victor raised his hand. Dexter just shook his head, but there was something rather cute about his boyish innocence. Sophia really wanted to get to know him better.

"What about the replacement for O'Neil?" Victor asked.

Sophia folded her arms as Addison stood up and smiled.

"I checked on them before I got up," Addison said. "The Council of Eight hereby refuse to announce a replacement until the killings around Mars stop,"

Sophia just smiled. It was great how Mars could pretend not to know what was going on, and implicitly demanding that the Empire stop their operations. Mars couldn't exactly claim to be better considering the amount of Martian Agents Sophia had killed over the years.

"Where do we start investigating?" Victor asked.

Sophia just smiled. "We start at where the enemy is starting. We have to go to the Solar De Costa Space Port,"

Sophia just smiled at everyone and Sophia could feel the excitement build within her because she was finally going back on a mission with her kill team.

And that was going to be great fun.

CHAPTER 4

The Solar De Costa Space Port was exactly what Victor imagined it would be like, it was massive, high-tech and extremely clean. The entire space port was about the size of more large countries back on Old Earth in a massive ring shape with hundreds of ships flowing in and out of the centre every minute.

To Victor it was a marvellous feat of engineering and timing and preparedness. He had researched on the ride over here the port and it was amazing to imagine if a single thing went wrong then it would have far reaching consequences for tens of solar systems.

Victor still wore his skin tight assassin suit and had activated its camouflage ability so he was as white and bright as the roofing he was sitting on at the very edge of the central ring. He could actually feel the heat coming off the ships as they zoomed off, and hear the humming, popping and vibrating of the ships.

Directly below Victor was nothing but a sheer drop of three kilometres and he seriously doubted even his assassin abilities would be able to save him. He doubted the others would have saved him given the chance, but at least Sophia liked him.

Addison and Dexter might have ignored him and focused on plotting the mission on the short journey to Mars. Yet Sophia had been kind enough to help Victor with some more training and she was asking… she was asking some rather strange questions.

She was asking about his sexual preferences, his past relationships and framing it in the context of relationships are dangers for assassins. But Victor just didn't buy it.

Granted Sophia was a hot woman and Victor had forgotten just how hot she was until she returned a few hours ago, but he couldn't be sure she wanted to have a relationship with him or not.

He had to figure that out.

"Come in Raven," Sophia said through the microchip in Victor's mind that all assassins had.

"Confirmed," Victor said. "No progress. Targets not in sight,"

Victor was rather pleased he had managed to be so professional and cold in that talk. He was getting better thankfully.

His mission was simple, as he was on top of the space port his job was to monitor the ships in case something was coming in or zooming off strangely.

Victor activated the magnifying ability in his

assassin suit and zoomed in on the ships below. All he saw were some dealers unloading grain, another ship was uploading up weapons for a shipment to a Battlezone and more ships were just filled with tourists.

The reason why he had chosen this position was because one of the structural weak points of the space port was a large beam directly opposite him. But Victor wasn't sure how someone would attack it considering it was cladded in diamond-coated steel. It was far from easy to break.

"Lioness, report," Victor said.

He heard Sophia quietly laugh in his mind. "Nothing in the departure area. Everything clear. No sign of known Anti-Empire targets,"

Victor felt his stomach twist. If there was no one around that pillar and in the departure area then Victor was really starting to doubt if this was a target or not.

Sophia patched Victor into another conversation between Dexter and Addison, as team leader Sophia could listen into everyone's conversations.

"Everything clear in the cargo area," Dexter said.

"Clear in the fuel area," Addison said.

"We should just leave this port and kill the Eight,"

Victor rolled his eyes. He hated Dexter.

"If we kill them now, Earth will have to impose direct rule and we can finally get rid of this Anti-Empire crap,"

"Sophia will never allow it, and it is against our mandate,"

"Fuck the mandate," Dexter said. "We need to keep the Empire safe,"

Victor was about to carefully ask Sophia to kick him out of listening to this rubbish but someone caught his eye.

There was a massive blade-like Annihilator class warship incoming. One of those ships had enough firepower to destroy moons and decimate enemy fleets so because of its size it made no sense why it would be coming in here.

"Annihilator Warship incoming," Victor said.

"Activate Emergency teleporters," Sophia said.

Victor pressed a button his assassin suit and focused on the warship getting closer and closer.

It wasn't even slowing down.

"Shit!" Victor shouted.

The warship sped up.

It was going to crash.

All the ships at the space port zoomed off.

The warship fired.

Victor teleported away.

Hundreds of thousands of people were slaughtered.

CHAPTER 5

Sophia couldn't believe what the hell had just happened. Not only because of the sheer amount of innocent people slaughtered for no good reason, but because of the power it would have taken to pull off such an outrageous move.

No one could simply enter an Annihilator Class warship, let alone order it to crash into a major, major space port. This was outrageous at the very least, outright treacherous at the very worse.

Sophia rematerialized after her emergency teleportation with the others into an old assassin safehouse that was carefully hidden inside a major factory. The safehouse was a rather harsh name for nothing more than a little silver box-room with bombproof walls, high-tech computers and plenty of weapons.

Thankfully there was only a single metre thick door that was the only way in and out of the safehouse. It sounded stupid to most people but given how the door outside was cloaked to blend into the wall perfectly. Not a single one of them had failed her. Sophia wasn't concerned in the slightest, she had been in hundreds of safehouses throughout her career.

This was far from the worse safehouse Sophia had ever experienced but it wasn't exactly cozy. It was barely big enough to swing a cat round let alone have four highly trained assassins inside, but Sophia had to admit it was amazing to see them all alive and safe and well.

Sophia hadn't realised until then how much she had been bracing herself for one of their corpses to teleport in. It was very possible, that had happened on two missions Sophia had led before.

Definitely experiences she never wanted to repeat.

"What the hell happened!" Dexter shouted.

Sophia couldn't disagree. This was about a million times worse than she ever could have feared. She had always believed she was dealing with a few rogue elements inside the council of Eight, but murdering so many people, destroying that much infrastructure and destroying an Annihilator warship.

That was big.

Sophia had little doubt the Inquisition, the most top-secret of the Empire's policing organisations, was already at the scene, the Martians were probably trying to help and the Empire Army would probably be sent in sooner or later to calm down (kill more like) any protests that started, because Sophia had a feeling what was really going on.

"This is a propaganda war," Sophia said coldly.

Dexter swore several times.

"Makes sense," Victor said. Sophia loved it how he was knowledgeable and thought about the bigger picture too. Something so few assassins considered.

"With members of The Eight wanting to separate from the Empire, they need to inspire the people and other Forge Worlds to agree to them. So what better than causing a massive attack and blaming it on the Empire?" Sophia said.

Dexter punched the wall. Sophia was almost concerned about someone hearing but these walls were so thick she doubted that was a possibility.

"We need to investigate the Eight," Addison said.

"Agreed," Sophia said. "Because of the attack they will more likely call a public meeting. We could meet, study and watch the members there,"

Victor shook his head. "Negative,"

Dexter looked like he was going to punch the lights out of Victor, but Sophia placed a hand on his shoulder. She was not going to let anything bad happen to beautiful Victor.

"Security will be tightened. They will want to play up the need for security because of Empire attacks. We need to investigate them whilst that's going on," Victor said.

Sophia paced around the safehouse. It made

sense, it was a damn good idea. With the members of the Eight busy spreading whatever lies they wanted, they would be far away from their offices. A perfect chance to investigate.

But why not kill two birds with one stone?

"Actually," Sophia said. "How about you, Dexter and Addison investigate the offices?"

Victor smiled, and wow it was such a beautiful smile. Sophia seriously wanted to see more of those.

"Okay," Victor said. "What will you do?"

Sophia shrugged. "What assassins do best. We sabotage,"

Dexter swore, and Sophia just wanted to punch him or something. It was ridiculous that he kept dismissing Victor, but she had bigger problems.

She was not going to let The Eight spread lies about the Empire. She had to stop them.

The safehouse shook. It vibrated

Lasers shot through the doorway.

The enemy was trying to cut into the safehouse.

Sophia didn't know what to do. They were trapped.

There was no way out.

And plenty of foes outside.

CHAPTER 6

Victor flat out hated the stupid pathetic ugly enemy. They were going to die.

The bright lasers kept cutting through the massive door and Victor just knew that their time was running out. There was no way out of the safehouse so they were going to fight their way out.

But it was stupid that the enemy had found them in the first place. These assassin safehouses were impossible to find, so how the hell did the enemy find them?

The door exploded open.

Victor leapt to one side.

Metal chunks flew past.

Armour cladded warriors stormed in.

Smoke filled the safehouse.

Victor laughed. The enemy were stupid. Assassins could sense their prey.

Victor flicked his wrists.

Holographic swords shot out.

He flew forward.

He swung his swords.

The enemy screamed.

His swords sliced them. Killed them.

Blood splashed up walls.

Blood splashed against Victor's back.

His friends were killing.

Victor kept charging.

Kept killing.

He loved it.

The smoke was thick.

His assassin suit activated heat sensing.

Large orange bodies showed up. The enemy looked confused.

They kept pouring in.

They kept charging.

They fired.

Victor jumped into the air.

His friends flew forward.

Dodging the bullets.

Something grabbed Victor.

Punching him in the stomach.

Smashing him into the ground.

Victor hissed.

Something slammed into his face. It was a fist. His assassin suit was blind.

The smoke got thicker and thicker.

His heat sensors were dead. They couldn't reboot. They couldn't do anything.

Victor swung his swords.

Someone grabbed his wrists. Icy coldness shot into him. Cold metal wrapped round his hand.

Snapping his wrists.

Victor screamed in agony.

His holographic swords snapped.

And as his attacker smashed their metal fists into Victor's head again, he just knew that he was beaten. He didn't know who had attacked them and won and broken his wrists, but Victor was truly frightened at what they meant for himself, the mission and his beautiful Sophia.

Just as Victor was about to slip into unconsciousness he felt a needle shot into his neck and Victor hissed. He felt fully awake and strangely enough his wrists were now perfectly healed.

When the smoke cleared a few seconds later, Victor quickly realised that the only problem was that his wrists and ankles were wielded to the metal floor by immense metal cuffs.

Victor slowly turned his head to look at the door and the immense smell of burnt oil filled his senses as he stared at a member of the Eight.

Of all the members Victor had studied in preparation for this mission, committed all their faces to memory and plotted secretly how to kill each and every one of them. There was one member he never wanted to come across.

From everything Sophia had told Victor about that idiot O'Neil, Victor had to admit that Joseline Masonic was far, far worse. All her humanity was dead, all her limbs and organs except for her brain had been replaced with cybernetics and she was standing right in front of him.

Victor just looked emotionless at her massive three metre tall metal body with thick humanoid legs, a metal beetle-like body and ten metal arms filled with rather terrifying looking instruments.

Of course Victor was never going to show this evil cow how he was feeling, but he was pretty terrified of her. He focused on her massive metal arms and wanted to scream as he saw some of the saws, DNA manipulators and chemicals she could easily inject into him.

Victor had no doubt whatsoever this woman had once trained with the Geneticists of Pluto. Those crazy men and women could easily transform a sweet little bird into a massive world destroying monster.

Of everything Victor had learnt about the history of the Empire, there was one quote a Plutonian geneticist had said to the Emperor himself that had always stayed with him. *In the end my dear Emperor, the only thing that separates your DNA and that of a bacterium is how it is sequenced.*

That alone scared the hell out of Victor, but at least the others had escaped. Victor really didn't want them rescuing him because a real assassin could always escape from any situation.

Victor hoped he was a real assassin.

But at least his beautiful sexy Sophia was safe and hopefully got away. He hoped that more than anything else in the Empire.

"Subject is a well-muscled man. Very strong. Showing no sign of distress," Joseline said in a computerised voice.

Victor wanted to kill her and he knew he would. He just needed to figure out how to escape first.

One of her cold metal hands slapped him around the face.

"Subject is fully alert. Experiments can begin,"

CHAPTER 7

Sophia completely understood where Dexter got the urge from, all she wanted to do was kill every single last Martian on this entire planet.

It was completely outrageous that those damn Martians dared to attack her, her friends and the safehouse. What the hell were those idiots thinking? Did they seriously believe they would get away with this?

Sophia sat on the freezing cold metal roof of the factory with the immense flat red landscape all around them. Sophia hated this planet, its people and everything about it.

Or at least she was just annoyed at herself. As team leader she should have been captured not Victor, not him with his amazing body, hair and smile. All the things and more that she just wanted to kiss, hug and enjoy late into the night.

Sophia felt the cold wind blow gently across her face and the smell of damp filled her nose, she had to find the Eight and deal with them forever.

Sure she wasn't going to be as reckless as killing all of them like Dexter wanted, but she had to understand what was really going on. Only traitors acted like this, Sophia had fought plenty of regenerates in her time, and none of them were this desperate to kill off pro-Empire forces.

"Area secure," Addison said.

Sophia nodded. She wanted to tell them she had a plan but that was before she knew the enemy was hunting them.

Now the element of surprise was gone. Sophia had always worked in the shadows, but now the shadows were rapidly disappearing.

"Victor is gone," Dexter said. "I noticed Joseline Masonic was there. He is as good as dead, and good riddance,"

Sophia spun round. "He is an assassin. He is our brother. He is not a waste of time like you think he is!"

Dexter smiled. "It was wrong of the Temple to allow a woman to lead our team. I was the born leader. I was born in the Noble Houses. I-"

"You are an assassin. An equal to all of us so get your head out of your ass," Sophia said.

Addison stood firmly next to Dexter.

Dexter shook his head. "Cows always stick together,"

"When this mission is over," Sophia said, "so are you,"

Dexter grinned. "I count on it,"

Sophia wasn't sure what the hell that meant but she was growing really concerned about Dexter's actions and attitudes. She was definitely going to need to be prepared to kill him, but she didn't want to.

All assassins were brothers and sisters. She never wanted to kill her family. But she feared she might not have a choice.

Sophia decided maybe, just maybe that the best course of action might be appeasement for a little while, until she could at least start to understand what Dexter was after or planning.

"Fine," Sophia said. "We leave Victor for now. He can handle himself and we head to Dragon Mouth,"

Sophia knew she had to go to the Martian Capital to hunt down the Eight, but she just wanted to help Victor.

As much as she was starting to fall for him (to her utter horror as an assassin), she knew that her duty had to come first. And if she failed there would be no Empire left for her and Victor to hunt in together.

She had to travel and leave him.

Dexter folded his arms. "That will work. The Eight will hold their meeting most urgently and I suppose for you this is good news. They will most probably take Victor there,"

Sophia wanted to smile but she didn't dare.

"Then he can escape and meet up with us there,"

Sophia said coldly.

Dexter just laughed and went so close to her ear, Sophia could actually feel his breath condense on her ear. She hated the feeling.

"I know you love him. If you interfere with my mission, I will kill him,"

Dexter took a few steps back and just glared at him. Now he had threatened her, Sophia knew he wasn't an assassin anymore. True assassins never disrespected their friends.

Sophia was going to end Dexter. She just didn't know how yet.

She just hoped she would have enough time to come up with an answer before he did something horrific.

But Sophia wasn't sure on that.

Not sure at all.

CHAPTER 8

Victor had never ever wanted to kill someone as much as Joseline Masonic. He absolutely hated how she had stretched him out onto a long metal slab and basically encased his hands and ankles in solid metal. He couldn't even feel them.

All Victor wanted to do was kill her and make her suffer for what she was doing to him. She had already extracted plenty of blood from him, almost so much so that he was starting to feel light-headed.

But thankfully assassins were trained to kill and survive and thrive with missing limbs, under the influence of poisons and much more. Victor never liked those simulations but he was grateful for them now.

Victor tried to look around the massive metal box-room he was stuck in with his annoying psychopathic captor, but all the walls were too smooth for his liking. He almost felt like he was trapped into a cube, a cube he was never meant to escape from.

The smell of burnt oil, harsh cleaning chemicals that stunk of lemon and burning sage filled the horrible air as Victor tried to consider what his best options were.

He felt the room vibrating and almost moving so he had little doubt he was being transported somewhere, so the choice was simple. He could either try to escape now or he could wait and just hope beyond hope that wherever this new place was, it would give him some much-needed options.

"Subject's bloodwork is most abnormal," Joseline said.

As her cold metal face stared at him, Victor just stared into her ugly bright red eyes. He looked forward to ripping them out sooner or later.

"Subject is studying me for possibilities to escape," she said. "Subject will be unsuccessful in finding any but it is assuming that the subject thinks it is possible,"

Could she honestly get any more arrogant!

Victor watched a small circular saw attached to one of her arms activate, hum and spin rapidly.

"I will now saw off the Subject's arm to conduct further more detailed analysis on the tissue and molecular level," she said.

The saw moved closer.

Victor had to think of something.

He couldn't lose his arm.

He had to save himself.

"I know where my team are," Victor said.

It was the only thing he could possibly think of. The saw moved further away, thank the Emperor.

"Subject is trying to stop me. It will fail," Joseline said.

The saw started to move closer.

It was moving faster.

Victor felt it closer to his flesh.

"I'll tell you the mission! Honestly!" Victor shouted.

The saw moved away.

Joseline punched Victor in the face.

"Subject keeps lying. Subject is an assassin. Logic dictates he cannot be trusted,"

As much as Victor wanted to say she was the one that was lying, he actually couldn't. She knew he was going to kill her the second he got free, but clearly logic was important to her so maybe that was his way to freedom.

The saw zoomed towards him.

"Isn't it logical to explain yourself to your captive before he dies?" Victor asked.

"Negative,"

The saw cut into his flesh.

Extreme heat filled him.

Colorizing the wound.

"It is logical to explain your logic to me. I doubt your logic is sound. That is a crime to Mars, isn't it?"

The sword stopped. Victor forced his face to show how deadly serious he was about his feelings.

In reality he had no clue if that was a crime to Mars, but he had a feeling her Martian beliefs were a little out there.

"Subject makes a valid point. The Logic Engine encourages sound logic and opportunities to test oneself. I shall comply with the subject's command," she said.

Victor just wanted to breathe a sigh of relief, but he held firm.

"Killing you, assassin, means preventing the Empire from having another blade in their armoury to stop us. My job is stop to Mars and Forge World from supplying the Empire what it needs for its war machine," Joseline said.

Victor pretended to nod along like this was all perfectly logical.

"Therefore," she said, "I shall do this by convincing the Eight to separate from the Empire. My Master will be most pleased and after the separation, Mars will stop supplying the Empire, bringing my mission full-circle,"

Victor shook his head like she was the most stupid person in the entire galaxy. Because anyone who hated the Emperor normally was.

"Why does the Subject believe I have made a miscalculation?"

"Because you idiot, you and your people crashed a warship into a space port. Thousands of Empire agents are storming this planet right now, killing me does nothing. In fact I have a suggestion for you,"

Victor loved the sound of the gears and computers and other mechanical elements inside Joseline's head turned quicker as she tried to see if he was telling the truth or not.

He wasn't.

There was only one thing he could do there. Give Joseline so much information that her computers couldn't handle it all and he had to confuse her.

"Take the inquisition. Hundreds of ships are here. Didn't your scanners detect them? Ours did. Just imagine how many spies, assassins and inquisitors are walking around your planet,"

Joseline looked annoyed at how.

"What about the Empire Navy? You destroyed what of their ships. They're going to be furious about that," Victor said.

Joseline shook her head. Hard. She was struggling to deal with all this information.

"What about the Pro-Empire elements of the Eight? They will be furious with you at these attacks. They are already probably trying to kill your friends,"

"What's your suggestion?" she asked.

Victor pretended to look so sorry for her. "You must release me. Think about it. I am the only person who can reason with them. You said it yourself I am a loyal assassin, let's trick them into helping us,"

Joseline nodded rapidly. She flicked her wrist in the air and the metal around Victor's hand disappeared.

Victor jumped up.

THE EIGHT

Joseline grabbed him by the throat.
Slamming his back into the metal slab.
Joseline smashed his head against the ceiling.
Victor's world went black.

CHAPTER 9

Dragon's Mouth was just as disgusting as Sophia had imagined. Sure she had been here a few times before on some different missions, but it was only now as she stood on top of an immensely tall skyscraper hundreds of metres above the ground that she was starting to really focus on the foul capital.

As far as the eye could see Sophia could see immensely ugly factories that endlessly stretched into the horizon, pumping out all sorts of toxins that were harmless to the humanless monsters of Mars, but Sophia was extremely glad her assassin suit protected her lungs.

For her lungs would probably be cancerous within seconds.

Sophia still smelt the faint hints of burnt oil, disgusting burning bodies and the very subtle hint of charred flesh from some of the factory workers that had mixed into the air. The entire planet was just disgusting.

The sound of cheering in the distance made Sophia's stomach churned as she knew exactly what was going on, a massive group of Martians were gathering in the central square around a large stage to listen to their foul masters speak to them.

As Sophia knelt down, took out a sniper rifle filled with high-velocity sniper rounds that could easily kill anything and carefully stared through the sniper scope, she wanted to shoot all these idiots in the back of the head.

She could have used any weapon given how assassin weapons could easily interchange ammo, but she needed the accuracy a sniper rifle gave her.

It was flat out stupid that they hated the Emperor and so blindly supported their Masters and the Eight. They were going to suffer for that.

Sophia activated the audio on her sniper scoop. She could now thankfully hear exactly what the six members of the Eight were saying on the stage.

She had no idea where the foul Joseline Masonic was, but that didn't matter at the moment. She would hopefully die in time.

"The Empire is going to wipe us out," a very large man said made completely from gold.

Sophia just couldn't believe how arrogant Harley Jameson was, he might have been in charge of the Eight and an extreme Anti-Empire spokesperson. But even Sophia wanted to believe he had more class than making his body out of gold.

"We must strike back now," he said.

Sophia just smiled. She had sent Dexter (with Addison as his guard and hopeful killer) into the crowd so they could create a distraction for her.

Sophia's only job was to kill the members of the Eight when the time was right. That was the mission now, but there was something wrong.

She had killed O'Neil a few weeks ago and no one had replaced him yet. That wasn't the problem, the problem was usually in all the video footage Sophia saw of the Eight they all spoke as one equal voice. Now Harley was the only one talking.

That was strange for these people.

And even though everything single member was made of metal and hated the so-called weakness of flesh. Sophia still understood that two members standing at the very edge of stage were shaking, nervous and really didn't want to be there.

Sophia didn't want to believe the Empire had some allies left, but maybe they did.

Sure Sophia had been briefed that not all members of the Eight were Anti-Empire, only a majority in recent weeks. So just maybe these two were the friends they needed to complete the mission.

Sophia watched the two members on the edge of the stage. They were both slimmer, acted more human and seemed kinder than the rest of the Eight. Sophia couldn't see them too much more from this distance but Sophia wanted to make sure she kept an eye on them for later.

"And we have proof of the Empire's treachery.

We will proof to you all! That the Empire can be stopped, and together we will hold the Empire accountable and stop them before they destroy us!" Harley said.

Sophia aimed her sniper rifle right at his head.

Then she noticed that the entire crowd of people below Harley were silent and looking at each other. No one exactly knew what he was supposing and even more didn't know if they liked it or not.

Sophia just grinned. Maybe there was hope for this useless planet after all.

"I give you. An Assassin!" Harley shouted.

Sophia gasped as she watched a heavily chained Victor walked onto the stage. There were chains around his neck, ankles and hands.

He looked awful, beaten and the Eight had just cut his head.

Sophia wanted to be sick. She couldn't confirm it but Sophia had heard stories of Joseline Masonic implanting some kind of mind controlling beetle into the brains of her prey.

Effectively mind controlling them.

Sophia just looked at Victor through her sniper scope. The crosshairs were directly on his head.

As much as Sophia loved him, Victor was a highly trained killer who could easily kill hundreds of people without breaking a sweat.

If the Empire couldn't have him, then the enemy sure as hell couldn't.

CHAPTER 10

Victor was going to slaughter each and every one of these Martian bastards. He absolutely hated being forced on that damn stage in front of all those silly Martians who were going to believe the lies of their Eight, go off into a war and be killed by the Empire.

It was stupid.

Victor hated the feeling of the little metal beetles crawling around his brain, controlling his every move. Victor couldn't even move a finger unless the beetles (and Joseline Masonic) allowed him to. She was definitely going to be the first to die.

If he could just damn well find her.

The crowd of awful faces that were dirty, stunk of sweat and looked so malnourished stared back at Victor as they tried to decide what was going on.

Victor wanted nothing more than them to decide he wasn't an Assassin and their masters were lying. But he knew that would never happen.

The beetles heated up his brain and Victor

screamed in agony. Blood trickled down his nose.

Victor knew the leader Harley was three metres to his left, the other members were in a line four metres behind him and that damn Joseline was safely away far from the stage.

"This is the disgraceful face of the enemy. He is weak. He is flesh. He is Empire!" Harley shouted.

Everyone booed and shouted at Victor.

Victor just grinned. This was funny. All these people were stupid, ignorant and pathetic. The Empire was hardly the true enemy.

Victor tried to move a finger but he couldn't. He felt the beetles heat up more and more as he tried to move.

After another immense wave of agony, Victor stopped. He couldn't risk getting brain damage from the beetles cooking his flesh.

But the real problem was he didn't know how he could get rid of them. He had heard the odd story about these creatures, she must have infected him when he was unconscious.

That fact would hardly help him now.

"This is why," Harley said, "I am currently broadcasting to all Forge Worlds. In a matter of two weeks every single forge world across the Empire will know my next decree as Head of The Eight,"

Victor knew he was going to announce the separation. He had to act.

Victor tried to move. The beetles burned. He couldn't do anything. He just knew the beetles would kill him if he tried again.

"I hereby announce Mars and All Forge Worlds-"

A bullet smashed into his head.

He didn't die.

Everyone screamed.

Victor surged forward.

Jumping into the air.

He wrapped the chains around Harley's metal head.

He pulled.

The beetles hummed.

They heated up.

His brain burned.

Victor kept pulling.

Harley's head sparkled.

It glowed red.

Victor was ripping his head off.

Someone smashed into him.

Punching him in the head.

Victor tried to block them.

The chains were stopping him.

Harley forced himself up. Running away.

More bullets fired. Smashing into Harley.

They reflected off him.

Harley was gone.

Victor held his head.

Blood dropped from his nose.

His vision went black. He screamed in agony.

Metal wrapped round his throat.

Victor tried to stop it.

He was too weak.

A metal collar locked on.

Something buzzed around him.

Victor's vision returned, and he was completely buzzed to see two massive metal people standing over him. Firing shots from laser cannons as Martian soldiers tried to kill him.

Victor had no clue what was going on, but he had a very good feeling that the Empire did have at least two friends left in the Eight.

Screams, shouts and orders echoed around the square. Victor wanted to fight but he couldn't.

His head was aching, his body was battered and his brain felt like he had been stabbed multiple times.

Victor had to recover.

He had to find.

He had to find Sophia.

The woman he loved.

CHAPTER 11

Sophia just stared at the horrible foul Martians in the little metal spherical chamber filled with its high tech medical equipment, computers and mindless servants helping them as the two members of the Eight worked on Victor.

Sophia really didn't like watching Victor lying on the cold metal slab completely naked (well that bit was hardly bad) with a strange humming metal collar around his neck.

Apparently the collar was a unique design to stop the brain beetles from working and receiving her commands. But given how most Martians were monsters, evil and soulless humans, Sophia wasn't too hopeful.

If Victor died Sophia was definitely going to torture these two before she killed them.

Thankfully Harley had been unable to give his command about separation, but Sophia just knew it was only a matter of time until he tried again. He definitely wasn't the sort of man to do it privately, but at least there would be another public opportunity to kill him.

Sophia was impressed at the strength of his armour and metal body. Sophia had stopped some superhumans were those sniper rounds, clearly (and very alarmingly) Harley seemed stronger than them.

Saying she was concerned was a massive understatement.

"Have your friends completed their perimeter check?" one of the Eight said.

Sophia just frowned.

After the attack Sophia had been pleased to hear Dexter and Addison had jointly managed to kill a member of the Eight, and they were checking for any surviving soldiers to interrogate (also known as torture) before they returned to her.

Sophia really wanted to believe Dexter was happier now, but she still couldn't shake the feeling that something bad was going to happen.

"Assassin?" the member of the Eight said again.

"They will return shortly," Sophia said coldly as the two Martians continued to operate on Victor.

She was extremely impressed when she heard them hum a tune and slowly pull the beetles out through Victor's nose.

Now Sophia actually had a chance to focus on the two Martians (she had been way too busy making sure Victor wasn't dying before), she had to admit her observations from her sniper position weren't that wrong.

Their bodies might have been completely made out of metal, but they had human eyes that still managed to give her such a sense of warmth, love and respect.

As stupid as it sounded Sophia felt like these two were no more threat to her than she was the Emperor. And after all, these two had killed some of their own soldiers to keep Victor safe.

That was beyond abnormal for Martians.

"For The Emperor," both Martians whispered as they stepped away from Victor and shot their laser cannons into the beetles.

Sophia was surprised they had such precision in those things that they didn't even warm her or Victor's skin.

Both Martians clapped their hands and the metal collar around Victor's neck dissolved and Victor slowly opened his eyes.

Sophia so badly wanted to rush over to him, scoop him up in her arms and kiss him. She wanted to taste those soft sexy lips against hers and then run her cold killing fingers down his abs and body, but she had to act professional here.

Sophia winked at him. It was about the only move she could afford him. Victor winked back and a very subtle smile.

The door opened behind her and Addison and Dexter stormed in holding a laser cannon he probably stole from somewhere.

Dexter punched the metal wall.

"What's wrong?" Sophia asked.

"The Eight's alive!" Dexter shouted.

Sophia just shook her head. Clearly that member Dexter and Addison had killed was still alive, damn these Eight were hard to kill.

Except O'Neil. Why?

Sophia looked at the two Martians. "Who are you both?"

The Martian closest to Sophia clapped his hands and the other one dissolved into a little cube of metal, no bigger than Sophia's foot.

"I am Lord Stanley Darley, Lord Commission of The Martian Army and Inquisitor,"

Sophia thought she was about to be sick. She was in the presence of an Inquisitor, one of the most powerful secret agents in the entire Empire. These people would burn entire worlds without anyone questioning them. They were that powerful.

"How?" Sophia asked, it was all she could get out.

"Stanley Darley was most interested in giving me his identity after he called me here, revealing he had brain cancer,"

"The only cancer you cannot get rid of by replacing it with metal," Victor said.

Sophia's stomach filled with butterflies. It was great to have him back.

"So Stanley gave you his body," Sophia said, "and what? You start investigating the Eight?"

Stanley nodded. "Of course. When I learnt about O'Neil I sent for assassins as soon as possible. Then I quickly discovered the conspiracy was far larger than O'Neil."

Victor stood up and went over to Sophia. She loved him standing next to him.

"You sent for us again I take it," Victor said.

Dexter stomped over. "He sent for us! Not you!"

Stanley shot Dexter a warning look. Slowly Dexter backed down. Sophia knew no one was stupid enough to challenge an Inquisitor.

"I sent for assassins to deal with the plot. My job was to keep investigating and find out who was truly behind this,"

Victor nodded and folded his arms. "When Joseline was experimenting on me, she mentioned something about a master,"

Sophia swore under her breath. It didn't need to be spoken that the traitors were involved, those evil humans and superhumans that sought to destroy the Emperor and enslave humanity. It was beyond outrageous that the traitors dared to influence and could actually get so close to Earth itself.

Addison stepped forward. "What about the cube man?"

Stanley laughed. "Yea. That was an android I created, it was a clone of a member of the Eight I killed,"

"They can die?" Sophia said grinning.

Stanley clicked his fingers and his chest opened

up, revealing five bright blue knives.

Sophia had never seen knives that strange shade of blue before and the material was almost mythic. It was smooth and rockery, like smooth jade, but not quite.

Stanley got them out of his chest.

"These knives," he said, "are ancient weapons that can destroy anything it touches. Even metal people. If you attack the Eight with one of these, then they will die,"

Sophia smiled. She reached for one.

Dexter whipped out his laser cannon.

Pointing it at everyone.

"Give me the knives," Dexter said.

Stanley looked at Sophia.

It was her call. She couldn't let Dexter go rogue. They were the only weapons they had against the enemy.

Sophia wasn't sure.

"Give! Them! To! Me!" Dexter shouted.

Stanley shook his head.

Dexter fired.

CHAPTER 12

Victor couldn't believe Dexter was being this stupid. Victor hated Dexter. He had to stop him.

Dexter fired.

Victor tackled Sophia to the ground. He had to protect her.

They rolled over.

Dexter grabbed the knives. He ran off.

Victor was about to chase after him but Sophia grabbed his shoulder, and Victor just knew that they had far bigger problems.

Despite the growing smell of charred flesh in the spherical metal room, Victor slowly turned around and hissed when he saw the completely charred, burnt and blistered body of Stanley.

"Shit," Victor said.

There was nothing else he could say, an all-powerful and dangerous and deadly Inquisitor was now dead. That was a crime beyond murder in the Empire, killing an Inquisitor was almost like killing the Emperor.

It was an unthinkable crime.

But as Victor stared at the disgusting body at his feet, Victor just focused on the wonderful feeling of Sophia's body warmth as she accidentally pressed herself into him.

Whatever happened, whatever Dexter did next, Victor had to protect Sophia no matter what. The Empire, Emperor and most importantly him, they all needed her alive.

Victor quickly realised another massive problem. Dexter had taken all five of the knives, only he could kill the Eight now, but even though Dexter had been an assassin for decades longer than him. Victor just felt like Dexter would fail.

It was why kill teams existed for these missions. Four assassins were unstoppable and victory was a certainty. Yet Dexter was a lone, crazy, rageful assassin.

He would make a mistake and die.

But what seriously concerned Victor was his own condition. He was more than grateful Stanley had managed to remove the beetles from his brain and managed to get his brain healed himself.

Yet he still felt a little weak, tired and like needles were stabbing into his brain. He had to be careful.

Victor just looked at Sophia. "We need to find the Eight first. Dexter will need help,"

"We have to kill him too," she said coldly.

Victor nodded. It was the law. He hated to

imagine how conflicted Sophia had to be right now, but the law and duty and the Emperor were her main concerns.

And he was going to help her no matter what.

"No!" Addison shouted.

Victor and Sophia spun round.

Victor folded his arms when he realised Addison was just checking out one of Stanley's high-tech computers.

"What?" Victor asked.

Addison slowly walked away from the computer she was staring at it like it was a rattlesnake that was about to kill her.

"Inquisitorial channels have scanned a thousand enemy fleets of superhuman and baseline-human warships three systems away," Addison said.

Victor just shook his head, that was unthinkable and what the hell would the enemy be trying to accomplish?

Victor knew that every single warship in the sector of space around Earth would be sent to destroy it. The traitors would lose within minutes, it was a pointless attack.

Unless something bigger was going on.

"What's the real issue?" Sophia asked, clearly coming to the same conclusion as Victor.

"The scans are spotty. No one knows where the enemy is constantly. We see them, they disappear and reappear next to another planet minutes later," Addison said.

Victor clicked his fingers. "If Joseline Masonic and the other members are in league with the traitors then they probably supplied them with something to cloak them better,"

Sophia and Addison were stunned into silence.

"That's why even the Inquisition cannot find that many warships. This device that the enemy has must be blocking out the scanners,"

Sophia nodded slowly.

"Why come here in the first place?" Addison asked.

Victor just frowned. "Because look at the direction of travel of the enemy. The first defences they will hit are controlled by Mars. The enemy can get within firing range of Earth long before they encounter any real resistance,"

Sophia swore in dialects Victor had never heard before. But he really understood her annoyance, this was one of the most outrageous and daring attack on the Sol System in thousands of years and it was all made possible by the stupidity of the Eight.

Addison's face went white.

"What's wrong?" Victor asked.

"It's a double-cross," Addison said. "The traitor invasion force will be within striking distance of Mars and Earth. The Empire's two most important worlds,"

"Fuck!" Sophia shouted.

"Mars thinks the traitors are allies as do the rest of the Forge Worlds throughout the Empire. Traitor forces will zoom towards all of them, and when the traitors are in range they will fire," Victor said.

Victor just laughed to himself because it was so simple, so clever and so cunning. The traitors were going to wipe out the Empire's entire manufacturing capabilities in the blink of an eye.

"We have a lot to do," Sophia said in a commanding sexy voice. "We need to kill the Eight, kill Dexter and find a way to unblock the scanners to reveal the location of the traitor invasion force,"

Victor smiled. It was a hell of a lot of work but it was going to be amazing fun.

And it made him more excited than any man had any right to feel.

CHAPTER 13

Sophia couldn't believe how badly this mission was falling apart. First the failure to kill the Eight, now an assassin had gone rogue and the traitors were basically going to wipe out the Empire in a single strike.

Sophia had to stop them all, and the streets of Mars were most certainly going to run with blood in the next few hours.

After thinking how she would kill the Eight as a rogue assassin (which was more than helpful because she had trained Dexter personally so she knew exactly how he thought), Sophia had decided the only way Dexter would kill the enemy was in the shadows.

And the only shadows and secret places left on Mars was the private meeting chamber where the Eight meet regularly, and were meeting now.

As Sophia finished crawling with Addison and sexy Victor through a very tight air vent with the awful smell of burnt oil, sweat and charred flesh filling her senses.

She popped open the metal grid that served as the vent's opening and they all climbed out.

Sophia and the others landed on a very cold metal platform that went round the top of the meeting chamber, that looked more like a grand cathedral from Old Earth than something that the Martians designed, in a large ring.

All three assassins knelt down on the freezing platform and Sophia focused on the five remaining members standing around a very large oak table with a hologram of Mars, Earth and the traitor invasion force above it.

This had to be one of the most disgraceful sights Sophia had seen in ages. This was treachery simple and plain, and there was only one punishment fit for that crime.

Death.

A blade touched Sophia's throat. The cold metal burned her skin.

Sophia didn't need to look round to know if it was Dexter. She didn't know if Victor and Addison were already dead. She just hoped they would survive and complete the mission.

"You have gone too far this time," Sophia said quietly.

Dexter hissed.

Sophia tried to look at how the platform was attached to the chamber. If there were bolts or suspensions of some sort then maybe she could bring the platform crashing down, but she couldn't see anything like that.

"I will not let you ruin this for me. You failed last time. I will not fail now," Dexter said.

He moved the blade away from Sophia's throat. Sophia stood up and looked up at him, she was surprised to see such a deranged hunger for death, blood and slaughter in his eyes.

Dexter was definitely a monster now.

He jumped off the platform.

Whipping out two of the blue knives.

He flew towards two of the Eight.

Then he stopped. He froze. He screamed.

Sophia quickly realised that he had been captured in some kind of energy field that immobilised any attackers.

"I don't think that was the plan," Victor said next to her.

Sophia wanted to ask where he had been and where was Addison. But she had a feeling she was about to find out.

But this energy field only complicated matters.

Dexter screamed.

Blood dripped onto the ground.

Sophia saw bright glowing shards of blue in his pockets and hands. She realised the Eight had just shattered the five knives Stanley had given them.

The only weapons Sophia had of killing the Eight were now destroyed.

And that really pissed her off.

CHAPTER 14

Victor was furious with the arrogance, stupidity and just flat out outrageous behaviour of Dexter. Because of his actions, the entire Empire might die, he needed those weapons.

Now they were gone.

As Victor knelt on the freezing metal platform above the cathedral-like meeting chamber, he just knew he was going to have to find a new way to kill the Eight. He just didn't know how.

Victor stared down at Dexter as he was caught in the energy field, twisting, screaming and in agony but the sound came from him. That just concerned Victor.

"Transmitting now," Joseline Masonic said.

It took all of Victor's strength not to jump down there and try to kill that evil monster.

All members of the Eight except from Joseline went to stand behind Harley Jameson and the large hologram of Earth, Mars and the traitor invasion force disappeared and focused on Harley instead.

It was happening. Harley was finally going to declare his treachery and that would start the domino effect of the Empire's death.

"Transmission travelling at full power," Joseline said.

Victor really hoped that Addison had managed to find the power cables like he had suggested, but he wasn't too hopeful.

He had to buy her some more time.

Victor looked around the metal platform and found a little chunk of metal about the size of a middle-finger.

He dropped it over the edge as far away from the oak table as he could manage. The chunk of metal hit the ground without sign of it being caught by the energy field.

Victor looked at Sophia. They were going to have to jump down too.

She nodded. They both jumped staying as far away from the oak table as they could.

Victor was fine. He landed with his back to the table.

Sophia hissed. One of her arms shot out. She was being dragged towards the oak table.

The energy field was larger than Victor realised. He whipped out a gun. He shot into the energy field.

It crackled. It banged. It popped.

It released Sophia.

Harley, Joseline and the other members just

stared at them. Victor looked back at their cold metal faces with no remaining humanity whatsoever.

Dexter screamed in agony. Victor's assassin suit hummed as it tried to block out the worse of the ear-splitting scream.

"Assassins!" Joseline shouted.

She flicked her wrists a few times and the energy field turned a bright white that showed a large constantly moving bubble around the oak table providing the Eight full protection from any assault.

Victor had an idea.

"We're in the Governmental building right. There's a mile gap between this building and the nearest factory, right?" Victor asked.

Sophia nodded. "Of course. Standard protocol in case attackers try to siege the Governmental Building,"

Victor laughed. "If we create a large enough explosion. We could annihilate this building, the Eight inside and not damage any factories,"

Sophia folded her arms. "How do we keep them trapped?"

Victor looked back at the Eight. He didn't know how. Clearly Joseline was controlling the field and it was a shame that Victor didn't have the technical know-how about how to create something to let him take over the field.

He wished Dexter hadn't been stupid enough to kill Stanley. He might have known what to do now.

The power turned off.

Dexter smashed onto the ground. He was too weak to move.

Victor's night vision activated.

The field was down.

Victor flew at the Eight.

The Eight hissed.

Sophia rushed passed him.

Addison jumped down.

The Eight attacked.

Victor dodged metal arms.

Metal saws.

Metal weapons.

Joseline shrieked.

The air hummed. Crackled. Sparked.

The Eight teleported away.

The energy field reactivated.

All the assassins were trapped inside.

CHAPTER 15

Sophia was getting outright furious with these Martians. If she was an Inquisitor then she would have ordered this entire planet to be exterminated and then these stupid Martians would understand the gravity of their actions against the Emperor.

As Sophia sat on the warm oak table and watched the bright glowing energy field around them, she couldn't believe how they had ended up in this situation.

Addison was sitting next to Dexter's injured body on the floor, and to her surprise, Sophia still didn't feel anything sympathy for him. He was a traitor and he was the reason why they were in this mess in the first place.

They were trapped. They didn't have any weapons that could kill these bastards. They couldn't do anything.

The only slightly positive thing of this entire experience was that the field energy was stopping most of the smell of burnt oil from reaching them. That only made Sophia more concerned about the risk of it stopping oxygen from getting into it.

"The field's too strong," Victor said as he poked, stabbed and tried to figure out more about the field.

Sophia just stared at him. He really was one of the most amazing people she had ever met.

She was a highly, highly trained assassin but she felt defeated, numb and just lost. But Victor was still fighting and that was very attractive.

All Sophia wanted to do at that moment was hug him, kiss him and explore his amazing body. But she just didn't have the energy to do much of anything.

Sophia had tried so hard to lead this mission, and she had failed.

Sophia looked over to Addison but she wasn't there. Neither was Dexter.

"Victor! Where are they!" Sophia shouted.

Dexter's maddening laugh echoed around the chamber.

Sophia looked dead ahead and saw him and Addison with their arms wrapped round each other on the opposite side of the energy field.

"How?" Victor asked.

Addison kissed Dexter. "You sent me to find the power supply. It was easy to find but I needed to go to Stanley's workshop first,"

Sophia's hands formed fists.

"You see my hubby and I," Addison said "knew Stanley probably knew about this field energy so he would have made something in case he ever got trapped,"

Dexter and Addison tapped on a shiny black bracelet they were both wearing.

"They look simple. Very effective though," Dexter said with a grin.

Both Addison and Dexter took off their bracelets and placed them on the ground so Sophia and Victor could only stare at their only hope of freedom.

A freedom so close yet impossible to get to.

"You cannot kill them!" Sophia shouted.

Dexter laughed hard.

"Dearest Sophia," Addison said. "Me and hubby don't want to kill them normally. We want to activate the nuclear reactors under this building. Bye, bye building. Bye-bye factories,"

"You're both insane!" Victor shouted.

Addison and Dexter made out for a few seconds and left.

Sophia felt even more defeated now than she did earlier. She had trained Dexter so well and Addison… she was like a best friend to her and Dexter but clearly they were more than friends.

Sophia had no clue when they had gotten married but given how crazy both of them were. Sophia had little doubt their marriage was just something made up in their weird little heads.

Victor sat down next to her. Sophia rested her head on his amazingly muscular shoulders.

"Well this is quite the failure. We're going to die

in a nuclear explosion. The Empire will die. We are such idiots," Victor said.

Sophia wanted to protest but that was exactly how she felt.

"Well, well, well," a very female human voice said.

Sophia felt shocked to hear a real human here. But she couldn't see anyone.

"I've seen a lot of people trapped before but for assassins I expected you two to be happier, more daring and more interested. You all look like idiots," the voice said again.

Sophia and Victor got up but still couldn't see anyone.

"You know my dears I could help you if you want. I could free you. You could kill your friends and the Eight," she said.

Sophia wasn't sure. It sounded too good to be true.

"Show yourself," Victor said.

A second later a very tall beautiful looking woman stood right next to the black bracelets. Sophia was surprised to see a woman wearing very thin armour, a long red cloak and holding an oversized shotgun in her hand.

Yet what Sophia was even more impressed at was the sheer aura of pure authority this woman gave off.

"Who are you?" Sophia asked.

The woman smiled. "Oh my dears. You must focus on your mission. I am not important. I just want to free you and you must kill your friends and the Eight,"

Sophia didn't trust her.

"What's in it for you?" Victor asked.

The woman carefully placed her foot behind the black bracelets as if she was about to kick them over to Sophia and Victor.

"I get to play in this building a little longer," the woman said.

Sophia just looked at Victor's handsome face. He looked so ready to kill everyone and complete their mission.

Sophia held out her hand and he wrapped his amazingly smooth fingers around hers.

"Fine then. Free us!" Sophia shouted.

The woman smiled.

She kicked the bracelets towards the field.

The bracelets slid through.

Sophia put them on. Victor did the same. They ran out.

The woman was gone.

They were free.

Sophia's reckoning was here.

CHAPTER 16

Victor was more than glad to finally be free despite how weird, strange and untrustworthy he felt like that woman was. But he was finally free to kill Dexter and Addison and the Eight. He could finally complete his mission.

Victor and Sophia each had a long holographic pair of swords in their hands as they entered the main reactor room with its massive ten nuclear reactors lining each side of an immensely long and tall room. It was probably the size of most cities back on Old Earth.

But Victor just knew that Dexter and Addison had to be doing something. He had checked the schematics of the reactor room on the way down and there was a large control panel in the centre of it.

Victor and Sophia kept moving through the reactor room. Their feet would normally echo off the smooth metal ground but the assassin suits made that impossible.

Victor kept checking their surroundings, making sure no one was following them or they weren't about to be ambushed.

After a few minutes, Victor pointed to a large holographic computer panel showing each reactor and Victor's stomach twisted into a painful knot. Clearly the two rogues had gotten here first and was doing something.

Victor and Sophia rushed over. Victor hated to see that each Reactor was being drained of coolant and the temperature was rising rapidly.

Dexter and Addison weren't just going to destroy the reactors. They were going for a nuclear meltdown.

They had to stop this.

Victor went to touch the holographic computer. Bullets screamed through the air.

Sophia tackled him to the ground.

Bullets smashed into the ground.

The assassins leapt up. Running for the cover of a nearby reactor.

Victor peaked round the corner. Dexter and Addison were walking their way. Their guns hot for their death.

Sophia pointed up. He nodded. Him and Sophia activated their climbing abilities on their suits.

The temperature increased. Victor started sweating. They didn't have much time to stop the meltdown.

Their fingers became sticky and they started climbing.

Victor hurried. Sophia flew past him. She was a great climber.

Dexter fired.

Victor dodged bullets.

He fired again.

A bullet shot his hand.

That hand lost its stickiness.

He couldn't get a grip.

A bullet hit the other.

Victor fell. He hissed.

He rolled onto the ground.

Charging at Dexter.

Dexter fired.

Victor was too quickly.

He tackled Dexter.

Smashing his fists into Dexter's face.

Again.

And again.

Dexter whacked him.

Victor fell off him.

Dexter kicked him into the stomach.

Kicked Victor in the balls.

Victor hissed.

Addison fired.

Bullets smashed into Victor's shoulder.

His assassin suit was struggling. Its shielding was failing.

Victor jumped up.

Dexter jumped into the air. Kicking Victor in the head. He fell to the ground.

Dexter jumped on Victor's chest. He was winded.

Victor tried to fight back. He couldn't. Dexter kept blocking him.

Addison fired at the reactor. Sophia was probably safe.

Dexter shattered Victor's nose. Victor screamed.

Dexter grabbed Victor's head and neck. He was about to break it.

Victor tried to fight back. He couldn't.

Shrieking filled the air.

A sniper round smashed into Dexter's chest.

Knocking him off.

Victor jumped on Dexter.

Snapping his neck.

Pounding his head into the floor.

Until nothing remained.

With Addison just frozen in what looked like shock more than grief for a loved one, Victor looked up at the very top of the reactor they had been climbing and Sophia stood there holding out her gun.

Victor loved it how assassin weapons could always interchange different types of ammo like it was nothing.

Addison charged at him.

Victor didn't have time to react.

Addison whipped out a knife.

Victor dived out the way.

The knife sliced into his leg.

Victor hissed. He punched her.

Addison jumped on him.

Slashing him with her nails.

Addison was furious. She was rageful. She would kill him.

Victor tried to fight back.

He was too tired.

Addison was too powerful.

He had to try

Victor rolled to one side.

Addison screamed. She didn't expect it.

Victor pinned her to the ground.

Addison headbutted him.

Victor's grip weakened.

Addison slashed his face. Catching his eye.

Victor screamed.

Blood run from his eye.

Blinding him.

Victor felt sweat pour down his back. The meltdown was coming.

His eyes managed to flick her.

Addison was raising a gun.

She was about to kill him.

Victor tried to move. He couldn't see.

Addison screamed.

When Victor had managed to wipe the blood away and his assassin suit had released enough drugs into his blood to help slow the bleeding, Victor was relieved to see Sophia standing over the corpse of Addison.

Given how much protection the assassin suits

gave them from jumping great highs, Victor had little doubt Sophia had leapt down and forced her blade through Addison's skull.

Victor quickly got up and rushed over to the holographic computer. He swiped a few buttons and managed to get the reactors to start refilling with coolant.

The temperature started to decrease.

There was no chance now of a nuclear meltdown.

Now they just had to find the Eight, kill them and find out how to unblock the scanners from the traitor fleet.

But Victor was amazed at how sexy Sophia looked standing over a dead body.

She was definitely one killer woman.

CHAPTER 17

As much as Sophia felt immense guilt over Dexter's and Addison's treachery, she couldn't focus on those silly feelings for now. She had to focus on the mission and how to kill the evil, foul, monstrous Eight. She just didn't have a clue how to stop them.

Not at all.

"Here," Victor said.

Sophia let Victor lead her through a very large iron door and into another cathedral-like meeting room like the one they had been trapped in earlier. Sophia still hated its awful oak table, smell of burnt oil and it was just horrible.

Sophia and Victor went into the meeting room more and drew out their long holographic swords. But something was off, it felt too quiet, too motionless, too much like a trap.

The Eight teleported around the table and Sophia felt an icy cold film coat her skin. Then she froze.

She was starting to really, really hate Martians

way more than she did before. She wanted to look at Victor to make sure that sexy man was okay, but she just knew that he was as immobile as her.

The Eight were going to pay for that.

Or more like five at this point, with O'Neil, Stanley and the member that Stanley cloned all dead, the Eight were starting to get thinner and thinner. Sophia just wanted to kill the rest.

She commanded her body to turn, move and react but it wasn't listening to her. She couldn't feel any of the beetles as Victor had told her earlier was having them was like, so the Eight had to be immobilising her another way.

Maybe it was because of a new technology, Mars seemed to be in an abundance of that. But she just couldn't move, she couldn't kill, she couldn't stop the traitor invasion force from coming here.

"What is it you hope you achieve here?" Harley asked.

Sophia felt the film coating her mouth move away so she could speak. She just didn't want to.

"I will not ask again," he said.

Sophia had to stall or something so she could think of a way to escape.

"You are fools," Sophia said.

The Eight started laughing, the sound of their computerised laughter was horrifying.

"The Subject is trying to figure a way out of the situation. She is useless against us. We cannot die," Joseline said.

Sophia smiled. "You can. You just didn't realise there were weapons to kill you,"

Sophia could hear Joseline's gears, computers and other mechanical parts of her work harder as she probably tried to confirm it.

"Impossible," Harley said.

Sophia felt like she could move a finger. Clearly whatever was keeping her trapped needed Harley to be concentrating fully.

"I killed O'Neil you know," Sophia said.

Harley frowned.

"Subject is not lying," Joseline said.

Then that got Sophia really thinking. Why had it been so easy to kill O'Neil but it was hard to kill the others?

Sure these people looked stronger, fitter and wore heavier metal than O'Neil but it had to be more than that. Maybe there was some sort of technology that was stopping her.

Perception and belief.

Sophia had always loved her days as an early assassin novice in the temple training, killing and learning things. Including the ancient Earth beliefs about the power of suggestion, belief and perception.

Her own Assassin Masters decades ago had told her in cryptic terms how technology was being developed to stop people from killing others if they didn't believe it was possible.

What if that was the key to everything?

What if this all came down to what Sophia and

Victor believed about their targets?

What if the film coating her was only allowing her to move a finger because she believed they could die?

"You are very, very moral," Sophia said with such conviction.

She felt like she could move an arm.

"You will die with your head on a spike!" Victor shouted.

Damn that man was smart!

"You will die by the righteousness of the Emperor!" Sophia shouted as loud as she could.

She broke free.

Victor charged forward.

As did she.

Sophia zoomed past Victor.

The Eight tried to defend themselves.

Harley teleported off.

Joseline did the same.

Three members left.

Sophia leapt into the air.

She swung her swords.

Slicing into the metal of two members.

Victor ripped the head off the last one.

Sophia slashed her two members.

She stomped on their heads.

She killed them.

With only two members left, Sophia couldn't believe how amazing she felt about herself and the utter thrill of the kill. She loved being an assassin.

"I was wondering how long it would take you," the woman who freed them said.

Sophia just looked at her and was impressed as she still looked so beautiful, clean and posh whilst Sophia and Victor looked dirty in their skin-tight assassin suits.

"How did you know? Why the hell didn't you tell us? Who the hell are you?" Sophia asked.

The woman smiled. "My dearest assassin I am an odd ball of sorts. I travel in the shadows. Do different things. Help different people,"

Sophia just wanted to punch this woman.

"Do you know where they teleported off to?" Sophia asked.

The woman's smile turned into a grin. "Of course. But if I tell you I need a little favour first,"

Sophia really felt like she didn't want to entertain the idea of a bargain with this sort of woman. But she knew she didn't have a choice.

"What?" Sophia asked.

"After you send the code to the Inquisition to unblock their scanners. Which I highly suggest you do in the next fifteen minutes. I need you to give me your word you will allow me to send my own message to the Traitor invasion force,"

Sophia and Victor pointed their blades at the woman's throat. She laughed.

"Believe me mortals. I am no enemy of the Emperor. I just need a little message to help the Emperor,"

Sophia didn't want to trust her but there was no other choice.

"Fine. We agree," Sophia said. "Just tell me your name,"

The woman whipped out a mini-teleporter, swiped it and smiled.

"The name's Oddballa. Sarah Oddballa,"

CHAPTER 18

Of all the things Victor expected to see when he, Victor and this so-called Sarah Oddballa woman rematerialised, he certainly had not been expecting to see Harley's body being hacked to pieces.

Victor drew out his two holographic swords as him and Sophia walked out on the massive jetty tens of kilometres above Mars's red ground and Joseline was kneeling on the edge of the jetty hacking apart Harley's body.

As Victor walked carefully over to her, he actually understood was she was doing. She was just as crazy, deluded and bestial as the rest of the traitors. He wouldn't have been surprised if she had never truly been a Martian or believed in their ways. She was probably just another spy sent in by the traitors to infiltrate the highest ranks of the Empire.

Now Victor kept walking towards her, all ten of her weird arms with all their instruments attached just laid there on the ground like they were powerless and dead limbs on an animal.

As he got closer, Victor was horrified to see how deranged she looked as she ripped open Harley's metal body and tried to eat the metal gears, wires and anything else she could.

But of course she didn't have a mouth. She didn't have a shred of humanity. She was nothing more than a mindless animal.

"What happened to her?" Victor asked as him and Sophia stood within swinging distance.

Sophia shrugged then they both looked at Sarah.

For the first time since meeting her (but even that was a very strong word. Encountering was probably better), Victor didn't doubt for a moment that this was the first time that Sarah was confused or she didn't know what was going on.

"Joseline Masonic," Victor said.

Joseline raised her head briefly like she was a deer who had smelt the faintest of hints of a predator and was considering whether to flee or not. Then she went back to trying to eat Harley's body.

Victor could see Sophia wanted to give Joseline a long speech about her vile she was, but they both knew it was useless. Joseline was nothing more than a deranged animal, she couldn't even understand what was going on.

Something major had happened.

Then Victor understood.

"The traitors," Victor said.

Sarah rushed over to Sophia and Victor.

"The traitors must have known Harley and Joseline had teleported here. Maybe this was a staging or extraction point if something went very wrong," Victor said.

"Then the traitors probably infected Joseline as a spy in case she ever got caught," Sophia said. "Maybe with those things like those brain beetles,"

Victor hated being reminded of them.

Sarah frowned. "That meant her brain's infected,"

Victor returned to Sarah. "You have a much better teleporter than we do. We need you to teleport to Stanley's workshop and find the device he used on me. He had to have a few hidden,"

Sarah looked like she was going to pretend she didn't know what Stanley was or what he did.

Victor shot her a warning look.

Sarah teleported away.

"Only a few more minutes until the invasion force enters the Sol System probably," Sophia said.

Victor bashed Joseline over the head. She collapsed to the ground. Then Victor carefully used his sword to slice open the top of her metal skull.

He was relieved to smell warm refreshing air came out of it. Victor started looking for any way to interact with her memory banks or something.

Thankfully because Joseline seemed to be obsessed with cybernetic replacements and getting rid of her flesh. She had gotten rid of everything including uploading her mind to a computer (a very illegal type of technology only the traitors had access to).

After a few moments Victor found something. A very small hologram projector built into her "brain".

He pressed it.

Nothing happened.

Sarah reappeared and handed Victor the metal collar.

He placed it round Joseline's neck. He pressed the projector again.

Joseline's entire mind was projected in hologram form.

"One minute," Sarah said.

Victor swiped it. Searched it. He found the technology send to the invasion force.

He found a way to undo it. He got the code.

Victor quickly read it out to Sophia who transmitted it uncoded to the Inquisition.

Seconds later the entire skyline was lit up with flashes of missiles, explosions and annihilated ships as the Inquisition, superhumans and other Empire forces open fired on the newly revealed traitors.

Victor felt a massive weight off his shoulders.

"Ten seconds later and we wouldn't be here," Sarah said with a touch of amusement.

Victor just looked at Sophia with her stunning hair, face and her perfect body. She was the most beautiful woman in the Empire and she was a great person. She could kill, make him laugh and smile and even now as they were kneeling next to two dead bodies, she managed to make him feel like a kid again.

She was perfect.

Victor gently caressed her cheek and she kissed him hard.

And he loved it almost as much as he loved her.

CHAPTER 19

Victor couldn't have been happier that the mission was over as he sat back on his metal stool at his large bright white kitchen table back at his communal apartment back on Earth.

As it was late in the evening, Victor had ordered the food replicators to make him a delightful fish and chip dinner with some of the crispiest most amazing fish he had ever had. And the chips were wonderful with their crisp outer shell and the fluffy deliciousness inside.

Victor and Sarah and beautiful Sophia had stayed mostly silent during the trip back to Earth, and that hadn't been too much of a problem because it finally gave him a chance to truly admire how stunning Sophia was, and how he actually felt about the mission.

The wonderful seasoning of warming spices filled the air and lingered on Victor's tongue as he wondered about what he would write in his report.

He would have to keep it emotionless, cold and calculated to prove he was a true assassin.

But deep down, he wanted to write about how exciting, thrilling and concerning it had been for him. He had loved the hunt, the killing of the Empire's enemies but he couldn't deny that he wasn't shaken by the entire thing.

The Empire had come so close to annihilation all because of the actions of one Traitor spy infecting the Eight.

Mars and Earth and every Forge World would have been annihilated without him and Sophia. As much as he was glad they had stopped them, he couldn't help but feel like all this could have been avoided.

Mars shouldn't have been so Anti-Empire and distrustful of the Emperor. Victor had double checked the history of Mars and there was still no clear answer.

But in Victor's experience even that was an answer.

At the end of the day in these sorts of situations, it was always down to the people not having decided something for themselves. It was all about leaders forcing their ideas onto their people.

So no. Mars was not Anti-Empire but because of Joseline Masonic's actions she turned the leaders into Anti-Empire puppets who then turned the innocent people of Mars into puppets too.

Victor had no pity or sympathy for the various

Arbiter (police) units and the odd group of Inquisitorial agents who were finishing up killing the Anti-Empire groups on Mars and on other forge worlds.

Victor's mission was done and he was looking forward to completing his training and being with the woman he loved.

The soft sounds of talking outside and the gentle footsteps of other assassins in the building made Victor realise that he truly was at home here.

Regardless of what his family, friends and idiots like Dexter believed, Victor was an assassin and he belonged here. Sure he liked to know how things worked, the bigger picture and other things that so-called traditional or real assassins didn't care about. Yet Victor did and this time it helped to save the Empire.

And Victor had finally achieved what he had vowed to himself only two days ago. He might not have trained much more, but he was better than Dexter. As a human being, an assassin and most importantly a friend.

Even if this relationship didn't work out with Sophia (which was extremely unlikely), he would always stay friends with her for a simple reason. Because out there in the depth of space surrounded by enemies your kill team is your only hope.

And Victor would always protect the woman he loved. No matter what enemy tried to threaten her.

Victor took another amazing mouthful of his

wonderful crispy fish and chip dinner and it was done.

Then Victor looked around the high-tech spacious apartment and was really looking forward to building a life for himself here, and using it as a base to serve his Emperor, Empire and soul mate.

Which was where he needed to go now.

CHAPTER 20

The very late evening sun glowed stunningly bright orange as Sophia stood at the very edge of a long metal platform high above the immense hive city below her. She felt the wonderfully warm evening breeze on her face, the sound of little pods zooming around her filled her senses and she was so glad to be alive.

As much as she utterly hated Mars for its people, politics and just how they acted. Sophia was relieved that the entire planet didn't need to be destroyed and rebuilt, Sophia had already contacted some allies in the Inquisition (no one had *friends* there) and it seemed that a new Council of Eight was already being created with trusted, very Pro-Empire beliefs and Sophia had read some of their personnel files.

Leading her to surprise herself.

Despite the hints of fresh, clean, crisp air being hard to get use to after spending so much time on Mars lately, Sophia was glad and actually felt that there was change on the horizon. As an assassin Sophia had been immersed in the dark seedy underbelly of the Empire for more decades than she ever wanted to admit.

She had seen entire planets burn in corruption, damnation and other stupid things because of the foolish behaviour of others.

And before now Sophia had always believed humanity would kill itself in the bitter end. Because if anything else humanity was a species filled with idiots and it seemed except for the Emperor, all the idiots were in power.

Yet after reading about the new members of the Eight, Sophia felt such power, relief and respect that the Eight would become a force for good again and that didn't see the Empire as the *other*, and saw it was an equal and part of itself.

Because that was the real problem at play here, the traitors, Mars and all the other people who wanted to tear down the Empire and what it stood for had forgotten a very simple lesson.

In the Empire everyone was equal.

It sounded silly from the perspective of history, and Sophia had met the Emperor once or twice and it was what he truly believed in. So why shouldn't she fight to do the same?

"You wanted to see me," Sarah Oddballa said as she teleported behind Sophia.

Sophia turned and smiled at the mysterious woman who even now looked so beautiful, strange and with an aura of authority.

"The Master Joseline spoke of. Who were they?" Sophia asked.

Sarah just grinned. "My dearest Sophia, your mind is sharp. Clever. Witty. But I will tell you something only me, the Emperor and very few others knew about the invasion force,"

Sophia leant in closer.

"The Lord of War himself was on one of those ships,"

Sophia had to force herself not to stagger back. The almighty, all-powerful leader of the traitors had been in the invasion force, that was mad!

Then it clicked.

"Was Joseline ever real? Or was she just made by the Lord of War and given so many memories that she felt alive and well,"

Sarah mockingly clapped Sophia.

"Of course my dear. Despite popular opinion the traitors don't have access to technology allowing a person to upload their consciousness to a computer. The Lord of War makes those people and he controls them,"

Sophia felt her heart stop for a moment. She had fought against one of the Lord of War's creations and lived. That was done very rarely these days.

"Then I assume Joseline was telling the truth about ordering the warship to smash into the spaceport," Sophia said.

Sarah frowned and nodded. "That was…

unforeseeable, even by me,"

Sophia folded her arms. "Who are you? I searched your name. Nothing comes up,"

Sarah gave Sophia a playful grin. "Because you are such a good sport I will tell you this. My message to the traitor fleet with spark a series of events that will either destroy or save the Empire,"

Sophia laughed. She didn't expect any other answer.

"Fair well, fair well and good-day my dearest Sophia," Sarah said as she teleported away.

Sophia's face lit up as she saw Victor in his sexy skin-tight assassin suit get off a cargo pod and walk towards her.

"What did she want?" Victor asked.

Sophia just waved him silent, pulled him close and kissed him. He was all she had ever wanted.

All Sophia wanted was to be loved, respected and seen as more than a killing machine. And Victor had given her that, she was definitely going to reward him.

Sophia wrapped her long killer arms around his waist and they both walked off together heading back to the apartment.

Because there was one thing Sophia wanted to do to him, and that was going to make her body and his feel the best they had for a long, long time.

GET YOUR FREE AND EXCLUSIVE SHORT STORY NOW! LEARN ABOUT NEMESIO'S PAST!

https://www.subscribepage.com/fireheart

Keep up to date with exclusive deals on Connor Whiteley's Books, as well as the latest news about new releases and so much more!

Sign up for the Grab a Book and Chill Monthly newsletter, and you'll get one **FREE** ebook just for signing up: Agents of The Emperor Collection.

Sign Up Now!

https://dl.bookfunnel.com/f4p5xkprbk

About the author:

Connor Whiteley is the author of over 60 books in the sci-fi fantasy, nonfiction psychology and books for writer's genre and he is a Human Branding Speaker and Consultant.

He is a passionate warhammer 40,000 reader, psychology student and author.

Who narrates his own audiobooks and he hosts The Psychology World Podcast.

All whilst studying Psychology at the University of Kent, England.

Also, he was a former Explorer Scout where he gave a speech to the Maltese President in August 2018 and he attended Prince Charles' 70th Birthday Party at Buckingham Palace in May 2018.

Plus, he is a self-confessed coffee lover!

Other books by Connor Whiteley:

Bettie English Private Eye Series
A Very Private Woman
The Russian Case
A Very Urgent Matter
A Case Most Personal
Trains, Scots and Private Eyes
The Federation Protects

The Fireheart Fantasy Series
Heart of Fire
Heart of Lies
Heart of Prophecy
Heart of Bones
Heart of Fate

City of Assassins (Urban Fantasy)
City of Death
City of Marytrs
City of Pleasure
City of Power

Agents of The Emperor
Return of The Ancient Ones
Vigilance
Angels of Fire
Kingmaker
The Eight
The Lost Generation

Lord Of War Trilogy (Agents of The Emperor)
Not Scared Of The Dark
Madness
Burn It All Down

The Garro Series- Fantasy/Sci-fi
GARRO: GALAXY'S END
GARRO: RISE OF THE ORDER
GARRO: END TIMES
GARRO: SHORT STORIES
GARRO: COLLECTION
GARRO: HERESY
GARRO: FAITHLESS
GARRO: DESTROYER OF WORLDS
GARRO: COLLECTIONS BOOK 4-6
GARRO: MISTRESS OF BLOOD
GARRO: BEACON OF HOPE
GARRO: END OF DAYS

Winter Series- Fantasy Trilogy Books
WINTER'S COMING
WINTER'S HUNT
WINTER'S REVENGE
WINTER'S DISSENSION

Miscellaneous:
RETURN
FREEDOM
SALVATION
Reflection of Mount Flame

The Masked One
The Great Deer

<u>Gay Romance Novellas</u>
Breaking, Nursing, Repiaring A Broken Heart
Jacob And Daniel
Fallen For A Lie

OTHER SHORT STORIES BY CONNOR WHITELEY

<u>Mystery Short Stories:</u>
A Smokey Way To Go
A Spicy Way To GO
A Marketing Way To Go
A Missing Way To Go
A Showering Way To Go
Poison In The Candy Cane
Christmas Innocence
You Better Watch Out
Christmas Theft
Trouble In Christmas
Smell of The Lake
Problem In A Car
Theft, Past and Team
Embezzler In The Room
A Strange Way To Go
A Horrible Way To Go
Ann Awful Way To Go
An Old Way To Go
A Fishy Way To Go

A Pointy Way To Go
A High Way To Go
A Fiery Way To Go
A Glassy Way To Go
A Chocolatey Way To Go
Kendra Detective Mystery Collection Volume 1
Kendra Detective Mystery Collection Volume 2
Stealing A Chance At Freedom
Glassblowing and Death
Theft of Independence
Cookie Thief
Marble Thief
Book Thief
Art Thief
Mated At The Morgue
The Big Five Whoopee Moments
Stealing An Election
Mystery Short Story Collection Volume 1
Mystery Short Story Collection Volume 2

<u>Science Fiction Short Stories:</u>
Gummy Bear Detective
The Candy Detective
What Candies Fear
The Blurred Image
Shattered Legions
The First Rememberer
Life of A Rememberer
System of Wonder
Lifesaver

THE EIGHT

Remarkable Way She Died
The Interrogation of Annabella Stormic
Blade of The Emperor
Arbiter's Truth
Computation of Battle
Old One's Wrath
Puppets and Masters
Ship of Plague
Interrogation
Edge of Failure
One Way Choice
Acceptable Losses
Balance of Power
Good Idea At The Time
Escape Plan
Escape In The Hesitation
Inspiration In Need
Singing Warriors
Knowledge is Power
Killer of Polluters
Climate of Death
The Family Mailing Affair
Defining Criminality
The Martian Affair
A Cheating Affair
The Little Café Affair
Mountain of Death
Prisoner's Fight
Claws of Death
Bitter Air

Honey Hunt
Blade On A Train

<u>Fantasy Short Stories:</u>
City of Snow
City of Light
City of Vengeance
Dragons, Goats and Kingdom
Smog The Pathetic Dragon
Don't Go In The Shed
The Tomato Saver
The Remarkable Way She Died
The Bloodied Rose
Asmodia's Wrath
Heart of A Killer
Emissary of Blood
Dragon Coins
Dragon Tea
Dragon Rider
Sacrifice of the Soul
Heart of The Flesheater
Heart of The Regent
Heart of The Standing
Feline of The Lost
Heart of The Story
City of Fire
Awaiting Death

All books in 'An Introductory Series':

Careers In Psychology

Psychology of Suicide

Dementia Psychology

Forensic Psychology of Terrorism And Hostage-Taking

Forensic Psychology of False Allegations

Year In Psychology

BIOLOGICAL PSYCHOLOGY 3RD EDITION

COGNITIVE PSYCHOLOGY THIRD EDITION

SOCIAL PSYCHOLOGY- 3RD EDITION

ABNORMAL PSYCHOLOGY 3RD EDITION

PSYCHOLOGY OF RELATIONSHIPS- 3RD EDITION

DEVELOPMENTAL PSYCHOLOGY 3RD EDITION

HEALTH PSYCHOLOGY

RESEARCH IN PSYCHOLOGY

A GUIDE TO MENTAL HEALTH AND TREATMENT AROUND THE WORLD- A GLOBAL LOOK AT DEPRESSION

FORENSIC PSYCHOLOGY

THE FORENSIC PSYCHOLOGY OF THEFT, BURGLARY AND OTHER CRIMES AGAINST PROPERTY

CRIMINAL PROFILING: A FORENSIC PSYCHOLOGY GUIDE TO FBI PROFILING AND GEOGRAPHICAL AND STATISTICAL PROFILING.

CLINICAL PSYCHOLOGY

FORMULATION IN PSYCHOTHERAPY
PERSONALITY PSYCHOLOGY AND INDIVIDUAL DIFFERENCES
CLINICAL PSYCHOLOGY REFLECTIONS VOLUME 1
CLINICAL PSYCHOLOGY REFLECTIONS VOLUME 2
Clinical Psychology Reflections Volume 3
CULT PSYCHOLOGY
Police Psychology

A Psychology Student's Guide To University
How Does University Work?
A Student's Guide To University And Learning
University Mental Health and Mindset

Companion guides:
BIOLOGICAL PSYCHOLOGY 2ND EDITION WORKBOOK
COGNITIVE PSYCHOLOGY 2ND EDITION WORKBOOK
SOCIOCULTURAL PSYCHOLOGY 2ND EDITION WORKBOOK
ABNORMAL PSYCHOLOGY 2ND EDITION WORKBOOK
PSYCHOLOGY OF HUMAN RELATIONSHIPS 2ND EDITION WORKBOOK
HEALTH PSYCHOLOGY WORKBOOK
FORENSIC PSYCHOLOGY WORKBOOK

Audiobooks by Connor Whiteley:
BIOLOGICAL PSYCHOLOGY
COGNITIVE PSYCHOLOGY
SOCIOCULTURAL PSYCHOLOGY
ABNORMAL PSYCHOLOGY
PSYCHOLOGY OF HUMAN RELATIONSHIPS
HEALTH PSYCHOLOGY
DEVELOPMENTAL PSYCHOLOGY
RESEARCH IN PSYCHOLOGY
FORENSIC PSYCHOLOGY
GARRO: GALAXY'S END
GARRO: RISE OF THE ORDER
GARRO: SHORT STORIES
GARRO: END TIMES
GARRO: COLLECTION
GARRO: HERESY
GARRO: FAITHLESS
GARRO: DESTROYER OF WORLDS
GARRO: COLLECTION BOOKS 4-6
GARRO: COLLECTION BOOKS 1-6

Business books:
[TIME MANAGEMENT: A GUIDE FOR STUDENTS AND WORKERS](#)
[LEADERSHIP: WHAT MAKES A GOOD LEADER? A GUIDE FOR STUDENTS AND WORKERS.](#)
[BUSINESS SKILLS: HOW TO SURVIVE THE BUSINESS WORLD? A GUIDE FOR STUDENTS, EMPLOYEES AND EMPLOYERS.](#)
[BUSINESS COLLECTION](#)

GET YOUR FREE BOOK AT: WWW.CONNORWHITELEY.NET

www.ingramcontent.com/pod-product-compliance
Lightning Source LLC
LaVergne TN
LVHW011844060526
838200LV00054B/4158